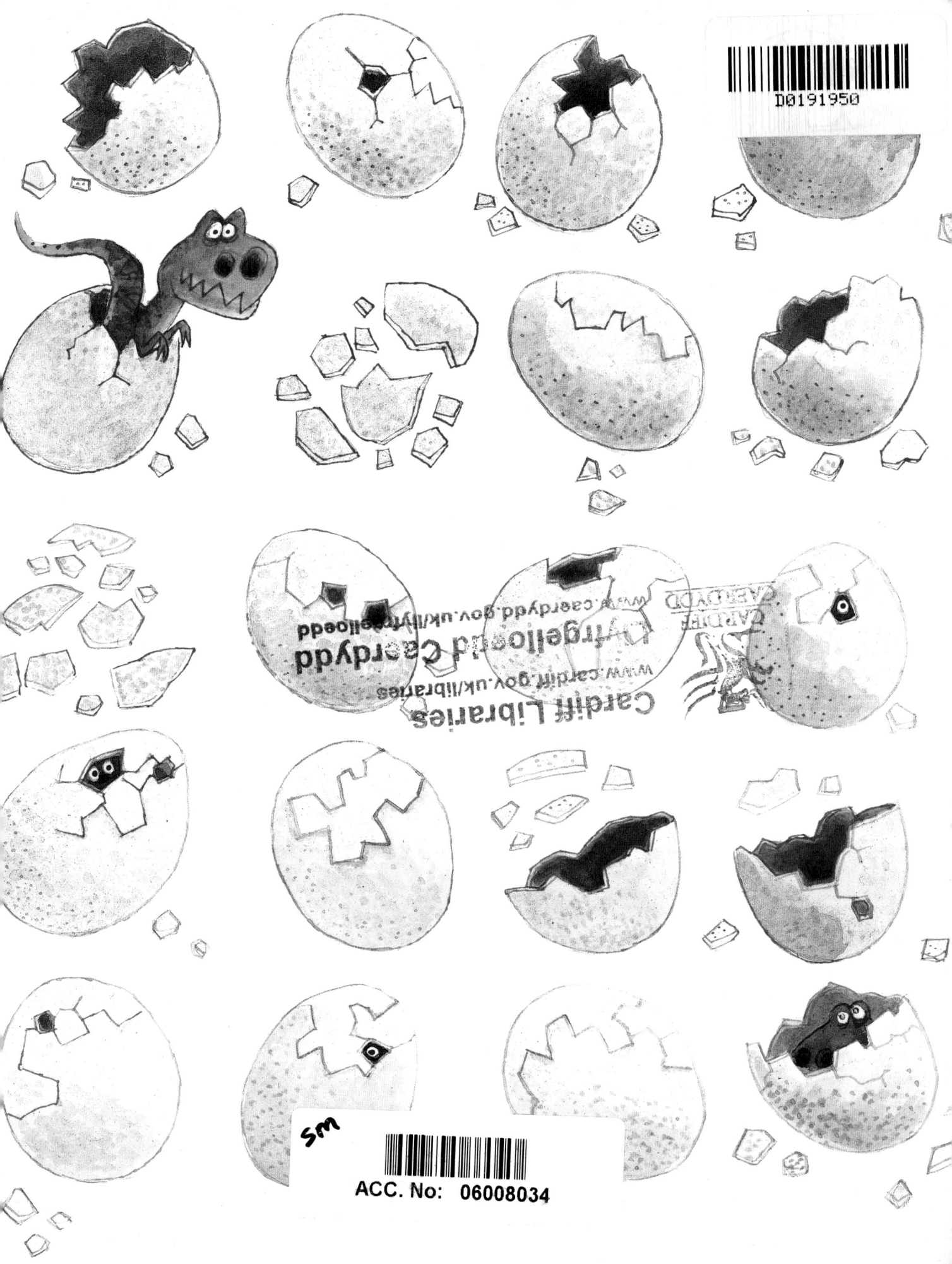

THE GREAT DINOSAUR HUNT

GRAA

HELEN FLOOK

Gomer

To Tyrannosaurus Alex and Brenda-saurus,
my two favourite dinosaurs – H.F.

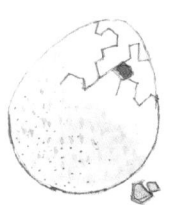

First published in 2017 by
Gomer Press, Llandysul, Ceredigion SA44 4JL
www.gomer.co.uk

ISBN 978 1 78562 198 7
A CIP record for this title is available from the British Library.

This book is published with the financial support of the Welsh Books Council.

Printed and bound in Wales by Gomer Press

Teddy and Pip were staying at **Gran** and **Grandpa's** for the day.

'We're going to **the museum**,' said Gran. 'What a treat!'

Boring! thought Teddy and Pip, but they didn't say anything.

But it wasn't *boring* at all.
There was a special exhibition on
all about **dinosaurs**.

TYRANNOSAURUS.

Teddy and Pip were **mad**
about **dinosaurs**.

They saw

dinosaur
skeletons . . .
dinosaur eggs . . .
and dinosaur footprints.

They bought **dinosaur hats**

and **dinosaur books** and had a *wonderful* time.

'Phew!' said Gran. 'That's enough **dinosaurs** for me. Time to go home.'

Back at Gran's they had 'dinosaur eggs' for lunch.

They **stomped**

and **roar**ed

and
chased

GRAA

GRAAARRRR

and
rough and tumbled

until Grandpa sent them out into the garden.

'Play quietly!' yawned Gran.

GGGGRRRRRRAAAA

Then she and Grandpa went
inside for a nap.

'Let's have a **dinosaur bone hunt**,' said Teddy. 'There must be hundreds of **dinosaur bones** in Gran's garden.' They found all the tools they needed in the shed.

'Let's get rid of these old **weeds**,'
said Teddy.

They both worked really hard until they had
a **huge** pile of *weeds*.

They **dug** . . .
and **dug** . . .
and **dug** . . . until . . .

'Look!' squeaked Pip.
'A **dinosaur egg** – just
like what we saw
in the museum!'

'I've found *hundreds* of **dinosaur eggs**!' said
Pip, happily counting his big pile.
'Me too,' said Teddy.

'Keep **digging**!
We must be close to the **mother dinosaur** that laid them!'

They **dug** even faster, until there were
ENORMOUS piles of **dinosaur eggs** everywhere.
'Hmm, no **dinosaur bones**, just eggs.'
Teddy frowned, stood back
and looked up from the hole.

The garden looked a bit of a mess after all their hard work.

'Listen!' whispered Pip. 'I think I can hear an **actual dinosaur!**'

It was **Granosaurus Rex!**

ARRRRRRRRRR!

But even worse, **Grandpasaurus Rex**, and he was VERY CROSS INDEED!

'I think I've gone off **dinosaurs** a bit,' whispered Teddy.

'Me too,' **nodded Pip.** 'Maybe we should take up

gardening instead!'

PIP   TEDDY

'Oh! Oh! I know!'
said Pip. 'Let's become
invisible!'

'Great idea!' smiled Teddy.
'C'mon, we'll start right now!'